Houses Floating Home

Einar Turkowski

Translated from the German by Belinda Cooper

ENCHANTED LION BOOKS
NEW YORK

ONE MANY

ORDER DISORDER

DREAM REALITY

SKY EARTH

NOISE STILLNESS

DESERT OCEAN

CALM IMPATIENCE

ROOT SPROUT

BOY GIRL

PAST FUTURE

One – Many

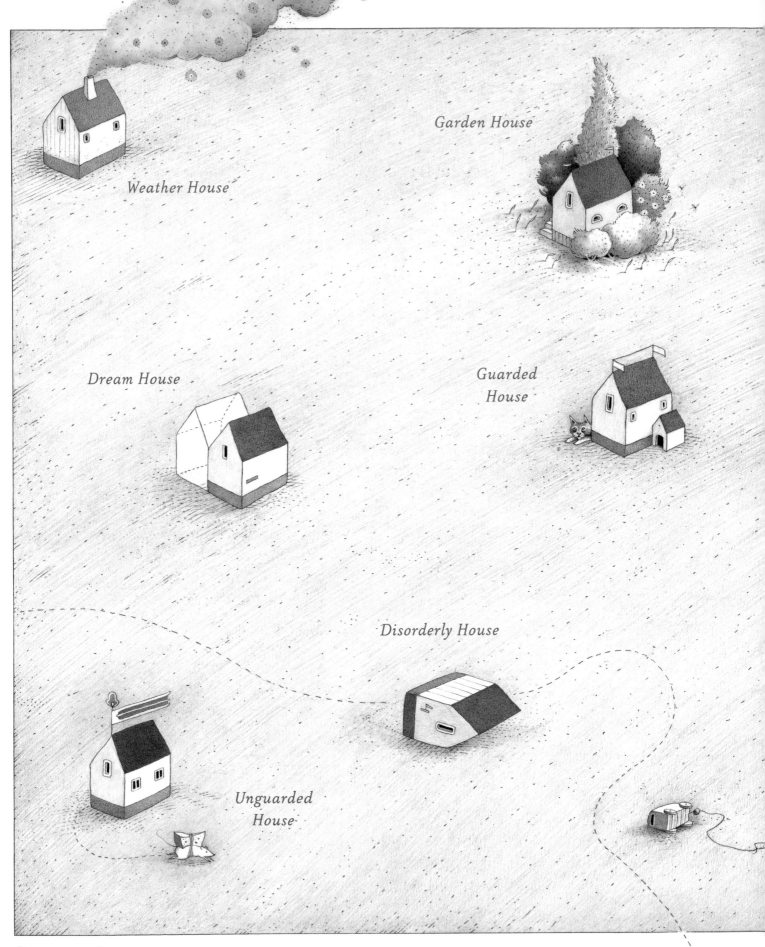

Weather House

Garden House

Dream House

Guarded House

Disorderly House

Unguarded House

ORDER – DISORDER

Bird House

Daisy's House

Tough Guy

Auction House

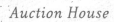

Beach House

Stairway House

Farm House

DREAM – REALITY

SKY – EARTH

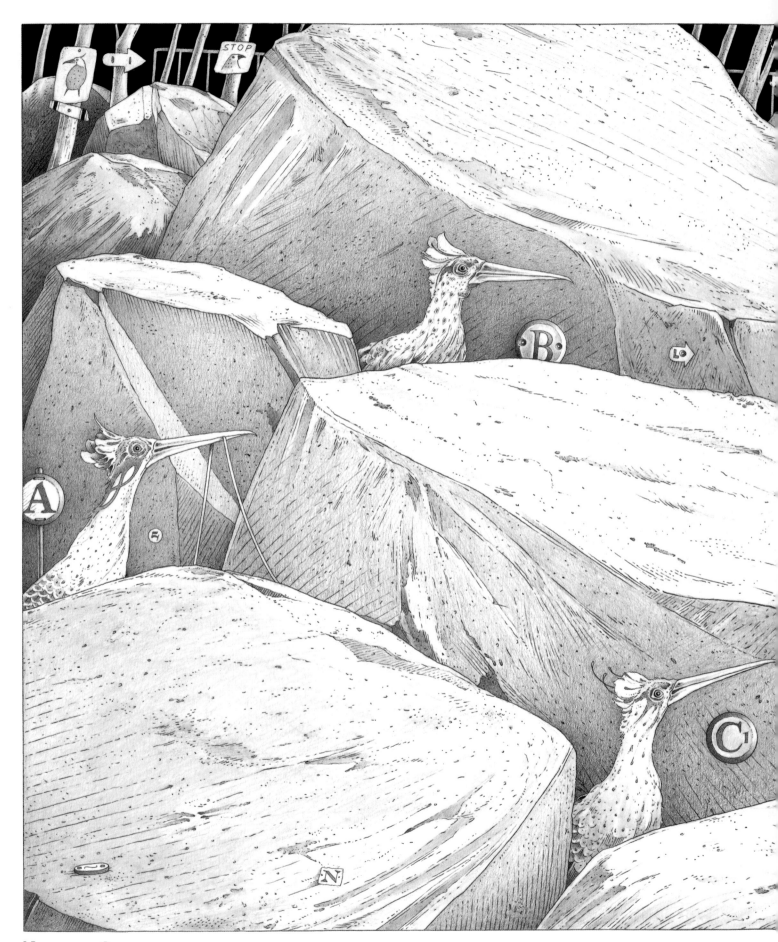

NOISE – STILLNESS

DESERT – OCEAN

CALM – IMPATIENCE

ROOT – SPROUT

BOY – GIRL

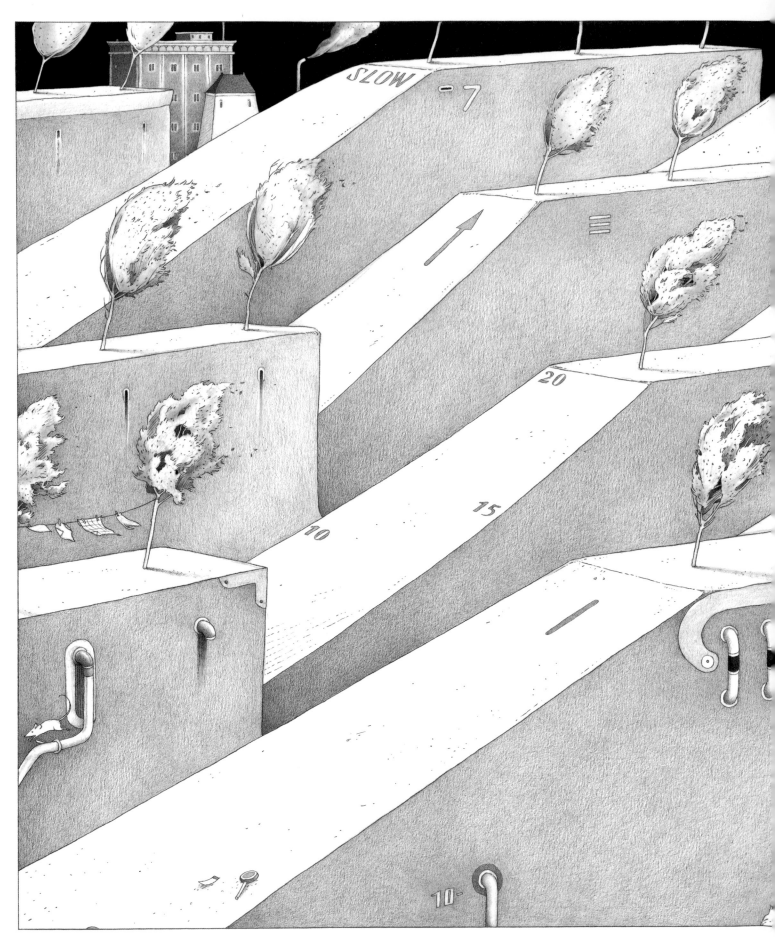

PAST – FUTURE

enchantedlionbooks.com

First American edition published in 2016 by Enchanted Lion Books,
351 Van Brunt Street, Brooklyn, NY 11231
Translated from the German by Belinda Cooper
Copyright © 2016 by Enchanted Lion for the English-language translation
Originally published in Germany in 2012 as *Als die Häuser heimwärts schwebten...*
All rights reserved under International and Pan-American Copyright Conventions
A CIP record is on file with the Library of Congress
ISBN 978-1-59270-183-4
First edition 2016
Printed in China by RR Donnelley Asia Printing Solutions Ltd.
1 3 5 7 9 10 8 6 4 2

EINAR TURKOWSKI, born in 1972, grew up in a small town near Kiel, Germany. His artistic gifts were apparent from an early age. He received his degree from Hamburg University of Applied Sciences, where he studied with Rüdiger Stoye. His first book, *it was dark and eerily quiet*, received many international awards, including Grand Prize at the 21st Bratislava Illustration Biennale and the Troisdorfer Bilderbuchpreis. Turkowski creates his work solely with graphite pencil. His books are loved around the world and have been translated into French, Spanish, Japanese, Korean, and Chinese.